Series 497

Beaky
the Greedy Duck

by NOEL BARR

with illustrations by
P. B. HICKLING

Publishers: Ladybird Books Ltd . Loughborough
© Ladybird Books Ltd (formerly Wills & Hepworth Ltd) 1950
Printed in England

BEAKY, THE GREEDY DUCK

This is a story about a duck, a white-all-over duck with a yellow bill and yellow legs. She lived in a farmyard with her six brothers and sisters, and she was the only white-all-over duck among them. She was rather proud of this and kept herself very clean and tidy.

Beaky spent most of her time on the duck pond. Sometimes she swam about on its glassy surface, admiring her reflection in the water, and sometimes she stood on her head and waggled her tail, but very often indeed she dabbled busily among the weeds at the edge, digging her beak into the soft mud, hunting for nice things to eat.

The white-all-over duck was interested in all that went on in the farmyard. Early in the morning she saw the cows as they came to be milked, and she watched them again as they followed one another back into the fields. They always wandered along so slowly, as if they would gladly linger in the farmyard. They gazed this way and that, rubbing their sleek sides on the gate post as they passed, and they stood and looked at Beaky and her brothers and sisters for a long time before moving on again.

A little later she saw the children, Susie and Jim, as they set off for school, with their satchels on their backs, and an apple or a piece of bread and jam in their hands. She knew when the calves were fed, and the pigs, and she knew too, that as soon as the farmer's wife had finished scattering the corn for the hens, she would go in again and bring out a bowl of scraps which she would carry over to the duck pond for Beaky and her brothers and sisters.

Now Beaky was greedy, and every day, while the hens were being fed, she took care to climb out of the pond on to the bank, and so be ready to get the largest share of anything the farmer's wife brought. The other ducks knew only too well that she did this, but somehow they could never remember to be there at the same time, and Beaky took good care not to remind them.

One fine sunny morning, the white-all-over duck floated on the clear water, watching all that happened in the farmyard.

It must have been a Saturday, for Jim and Susie were not at school, they were playing near the pump. Susie was having a grand wash of all her dolls' clothes, and Jim was sailing paper boats in the trough. Beaky saw their mother carry pails of milk to the calves in the paddock, and after that she watched her go to the pigs, and then back into the house again. She clapped her beak and waggled her tail. Soon the hens would be fed, and after that ! . .

Beaky was so excited that she swam round and round in circles and then turned upside down, head deep in the water, white tail uppermost. Up she bobbed, and now she saw the farmer's wife come out, bowl in hand. " Good ! " Beaky quacked. " Good ! hens now, ducks next ! " and again she rushed round and round, and then dived. But when she lifted her head this time, what did she see ! The farmer's wife had left the hens until afterwards, and was just beginning to scatter the scraps on the grass by the pond,

and all Beaky's relations were waddling towards her in a line !

How Beaky hurried then! Her yellow legs went like paddles in the water, her tail shook from side to side, and in a flurry of splashes with neck outstretched, she reached the bank, and began to climb out. But . . . oh dear . . . this was not the place at which she usually left the pond, it was nothing but black sticky mud ! Her feet slid from under her again and again, and when at last she managed to struggle out on to the grass, her beautiful white breast, her yellow bill, and her yellow legs were covered all over with black mud !

There she stood, a sorry little figure. The farmer's wife laughed, and threw the last scrap at her, telling her she looked like a little sweep, and her brothers and sisters, busy gobbling, quacked rudely at her, and said she had got what she deserved at last, and it was a pity she couldn't see what a fright she looked. And they laughed at her, and told her the mud would never come off !

Beaky felt dreadful ! Perhaps it served her right for being such a greedy little duck, and always wanting the best for herself, but she couldn't bear to be laughed

at, and she hated being so dirty. She felt she must get away by herself until the other ducks had forgotten all about it, and she had managed to make herself white again. Strangely enough she didn't think of going straight back into the water, and washing off the mud; instead she ran with flapping wings past the farmer's wife, and on towards the haystack, with some idea of hiding behind it.

But Beaky's troubles were by no means over. She squeaked so noisily as she ran that Susie and Jim looked up to see what was happening.

As soon as Jim saw the dirty little duck he gave a shout and pounced on her, carrying her back in triumph to Susie at the pump.

" Look ! " he said with a chuckle. " Look at this funny little duck ! She's been a little too quick this time ! We must wash her ! " And thereupon Beaky was plunged into the trough and held there firmly by Jim while Susie rubbed and scrubbed all the mud off her.

" Now don't get into that state again," Susie said, shaking her finger at her. " Jim,

I think she must be punished for being so greedy that she gets herself covered with mud. She must wear a pinafore to keep her clean."

So Beaky was put into a blue and white checked doll's pinafore which was tied at the back of her neck so that she couldn't possibly take it off by herself, and then she was put on her feet and allowed to go.

And now it was really poor Beaky, for as she shambled off, almost tripping over the pinafore, she was greeted from all sides by grunts and snorts and squeaks of amusement, and she found herself followed

by a little procession of cheeky chickens and a grinning farmyard cat, while three of four little pink pigs stopped digging under the hedge and came tumbling out, to stand and call after her.

The white-all-over duck felt terribly ashamed, and didn't know what to do. She felt more than ever that she must get away and hide, and somehow—somehow get rid of the horrid pinafore. She couldn't go to the pond again, for her brothers and sisters would tease her unmercifully.

She hurried on as quickly as she could in the blue and white pinafore, still followed by the jeering crowd, until she came to the door of the barn. It was open just a little way, and Beaky squeezed herself through, hoping and hoping that no one would follow her.

It was dark and dusty in the barn, and there was a smell of hay. Beaky stumbled over into a corner, her eyes on the streak of light coming through the almost shut door. No, no one followed her—how glad she was and soon her heart stopped thumping so hard.

She stood in her corner, glad to be alone. Then her little white head dropped lower and lower on her breast, while a tear trickled out of each of her little yellow eyes, and rolled off the end of her beak.

This hateful pinafore ! What was she to do about it ? She stopped crying, and turning her head, tried to peck the bow at the back of her neck. It was hopeless, she couldn't get anywhere near it. She would have to wear it always, she thought to herself, and at this her tears flowed once more.

She could never go out of the barn again—she would have to stay there, and perhaps starve to death !

The thought of all this made Beaky feel worse than ever, and she was just going to cry really hard, when she heard a sound in the rafters above her head, and a voice said, " Anything wrong ? "

Beaky was very startled, and looked up quickly. She tried to answer, but only a sobbing kind of noise came. Next moment a big brown owl dropped silently down beside her.

"What's all this?" he asked, gazing at Beaky with great round eyes. First he looked at the check pinafore, and after that at the tears rolling down the little duck's beak, and then he gave a funny little choke.

The white-all-over duck wasn't at all sure whether the owl was cross with her for disturbing him, or whether he was going to be kind.

In any case, she didn't really care which it was, she was so glad to think that there was someone who didn't laugh at her. She told the owl all that had happened, and she told it quite truly, too, admitting that it had all come about through her own greediness.

" H'm," said the owl, when Beaky had finished. " H'm, you deserve all you got, you know. People who live in farmyards have to play fair."

" Yes," the duck answered, in a very small voice. " I don't think I shall ever be greedy again. You . . . er . . . wouldn't be kind enough to undo this knot for me, would you, Mr. Owl? I could never go into the farmyard again, wearing this. Will you help me, please ? "

" Well," said the brown owl, his round eyes still staring at Beaky, " I think you've learnt your lesson, so I'll try to get it off for you. I'll take it to my wife, she'll use it for keeping the children warm. Turn round! "

Beaky turned her back to the owl, and then there began such a struggle ! The owl's sharp beak pecked at the bow, he may have been a very wise bird, but he knew nothing about a bow, and of course it didn't occur to him to pull one of the long ends. He worked and worked at it, and sometimes he pecked the bow, and sometimes he pecked the back of Beaky's neck. It was difficult not to squawk when this happened, but Beaky kept her bill tightly shut, and only squawked inside herself.

At last it was done, and the pinafore fell in a little circle round the white-all-over duck's feet. She stepped out of it with a

great sigh of relief, and thanked the owl over and over again.

" There's a hole over there by the corn bin," said the owl. " You can get down to the pond without crossing the yard, if you go that way." How thankful Beaky was when she heard that.

" Oh, Mr. Owl," she said. " I don't know WHAT I should have done without you ! Will you look just inside this hole every morning ? "

"All right," answered the owl, "but what for ? Now mind, you've promised not to be greedy again. Goodbye ! " And picking up the doll's pinafore by its frill, he flew up again into the dim roof of the barn.

Beaky looked carefully through the hole, saw no one, and rushed, using wings as well as feet, to the pond. Her brothers and sisters were at the other end, and were too busy among the weeds to do much more than gabble at her but, flat on the grass, dabbling their hands in the water, were Susie and Jim.

" Look, there's the white duck ! " cried Susie. " What has she done with the pinafore ? It must have come undone! " Little did she think that it had gone to keep the owl's children warm.

. . . .

Ever afterwards, as long as the brown owl lived in the barn, Beaky saved the largest crusts she could find among her share of the scraps, and put them carefully inside the hole at the back of the barn.

Series 497